Yuck Soup

Story by

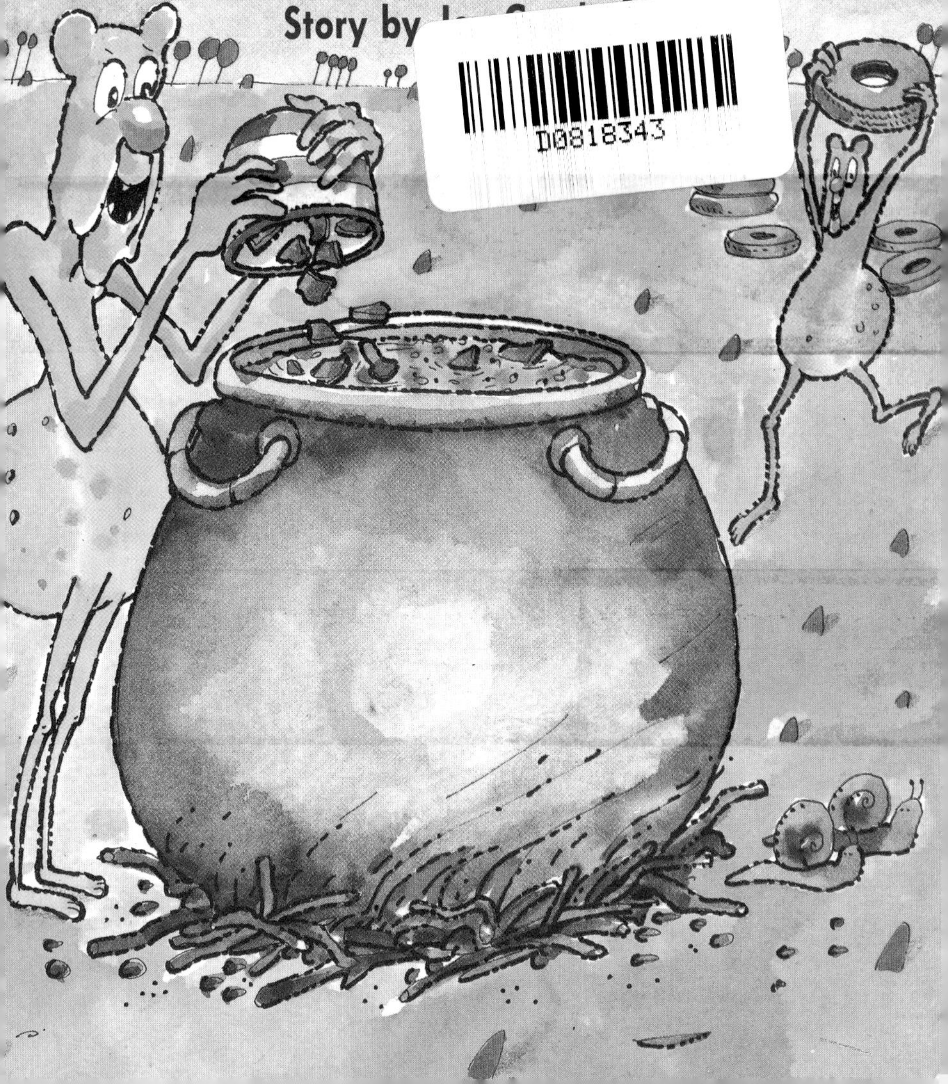

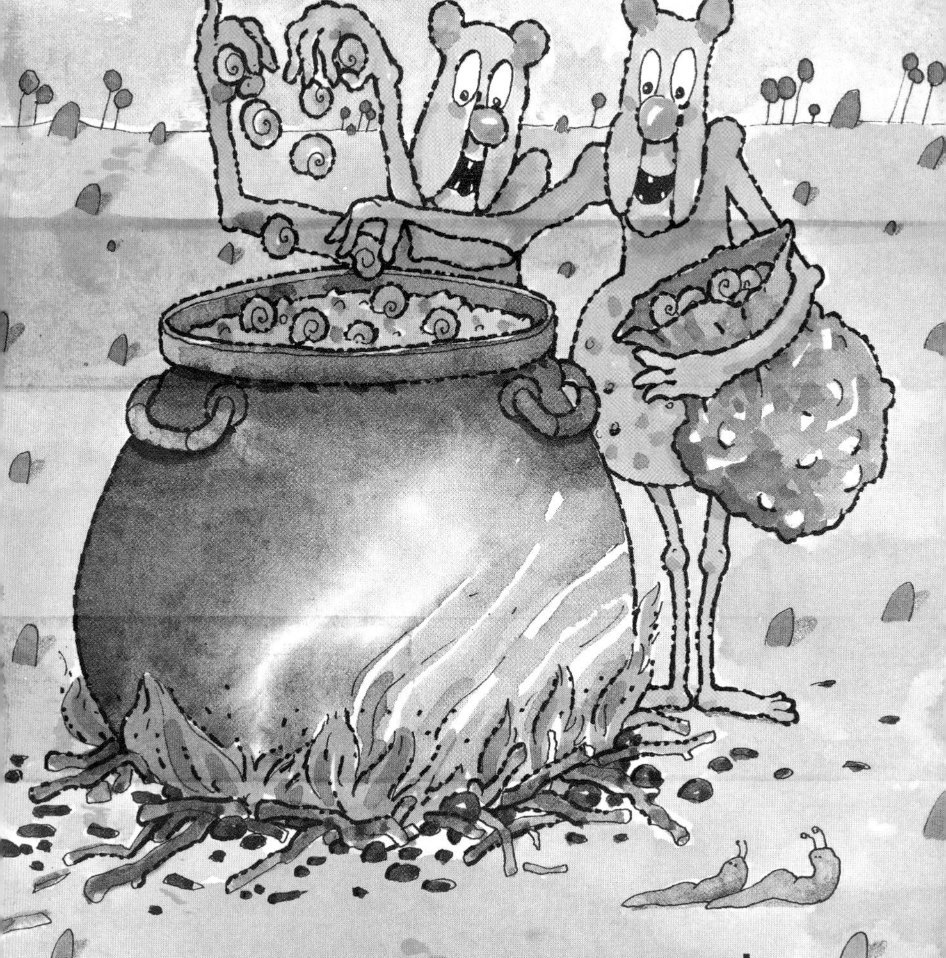

In go some snails.

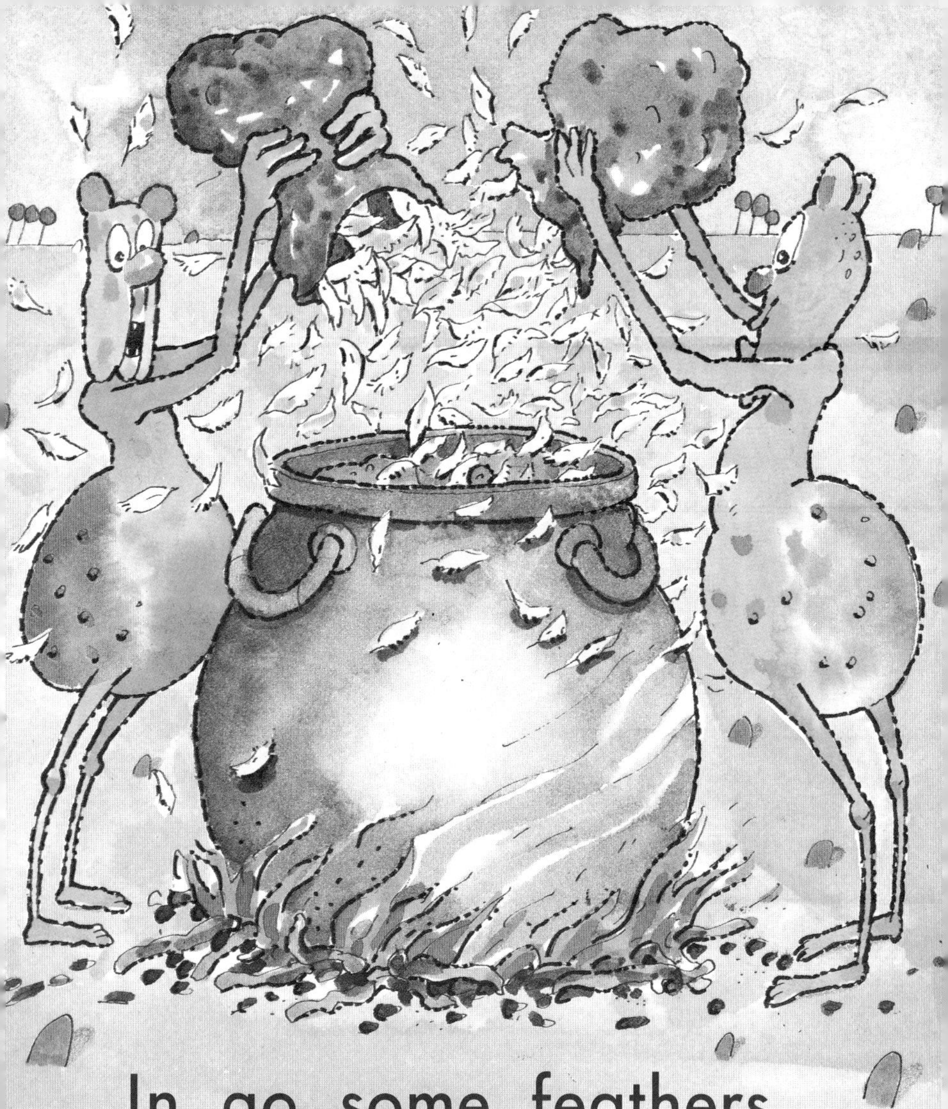

In go some feathers.

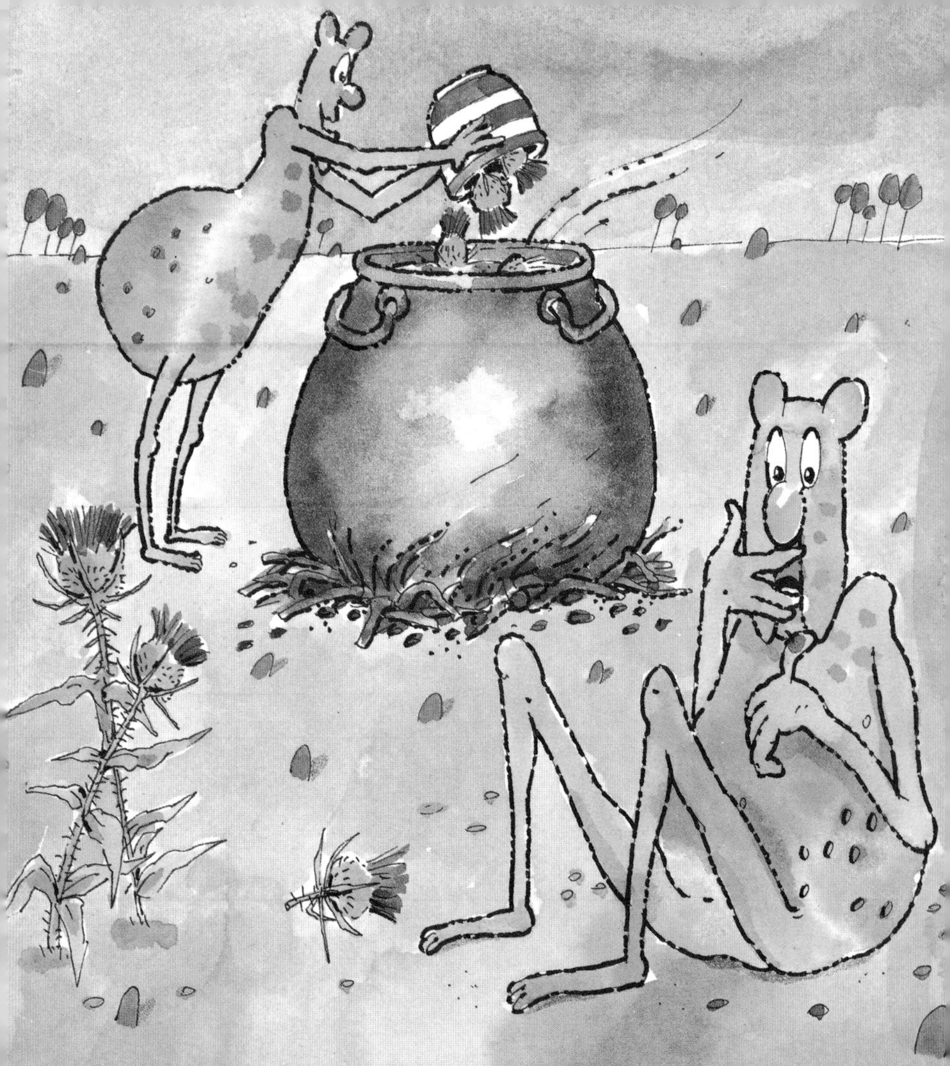

In go some thistles.

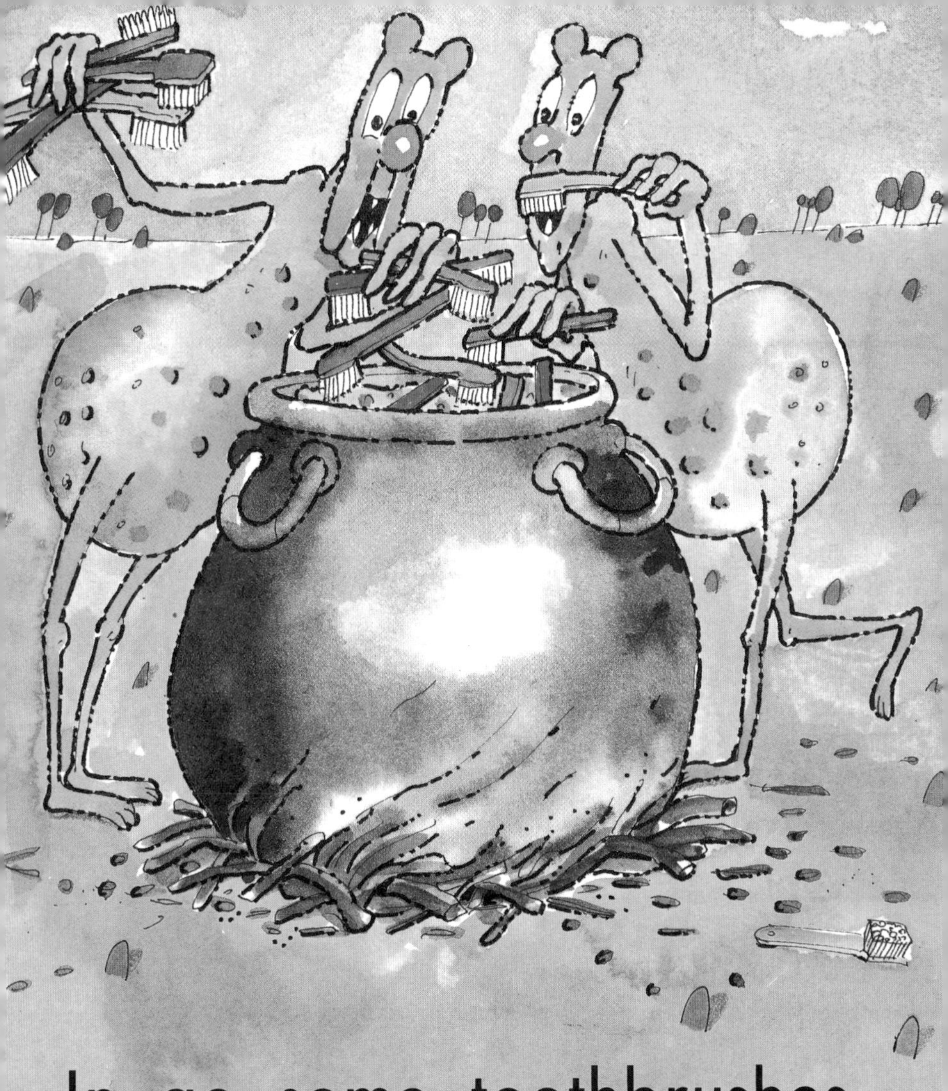

In go some toothbrushes.

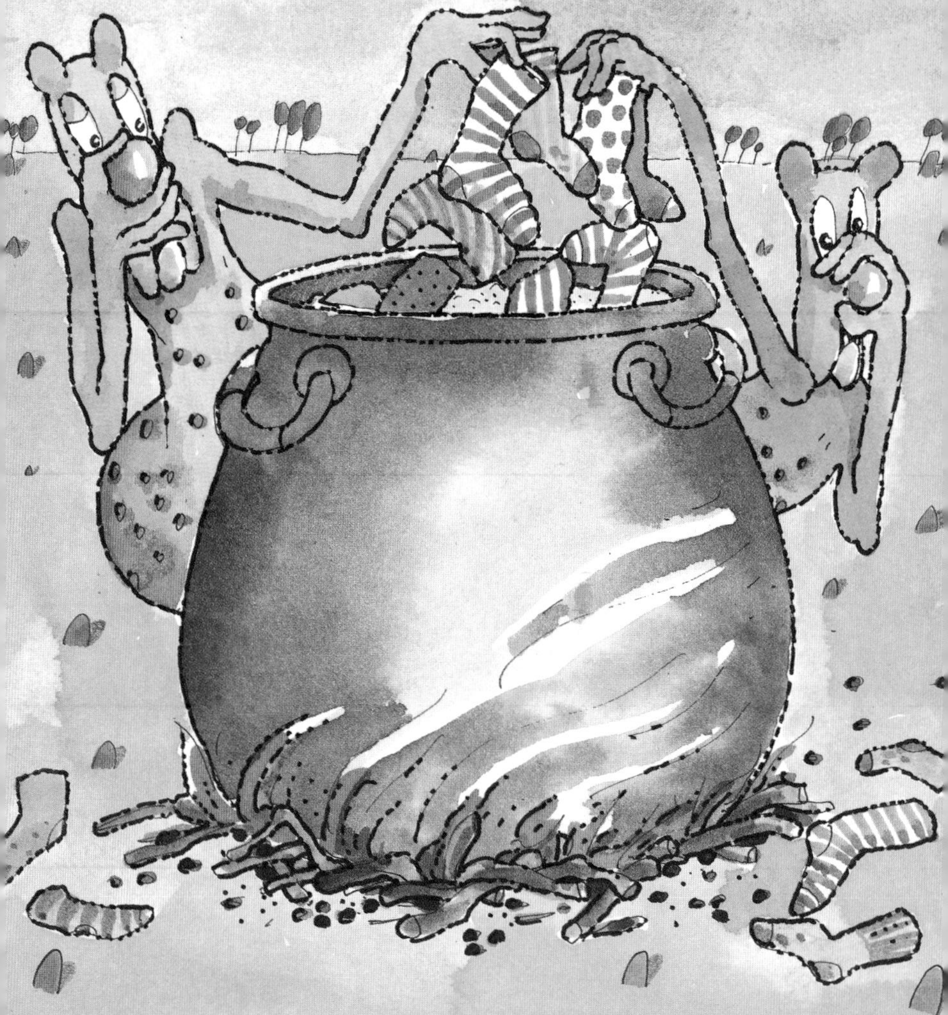

In go some socks.

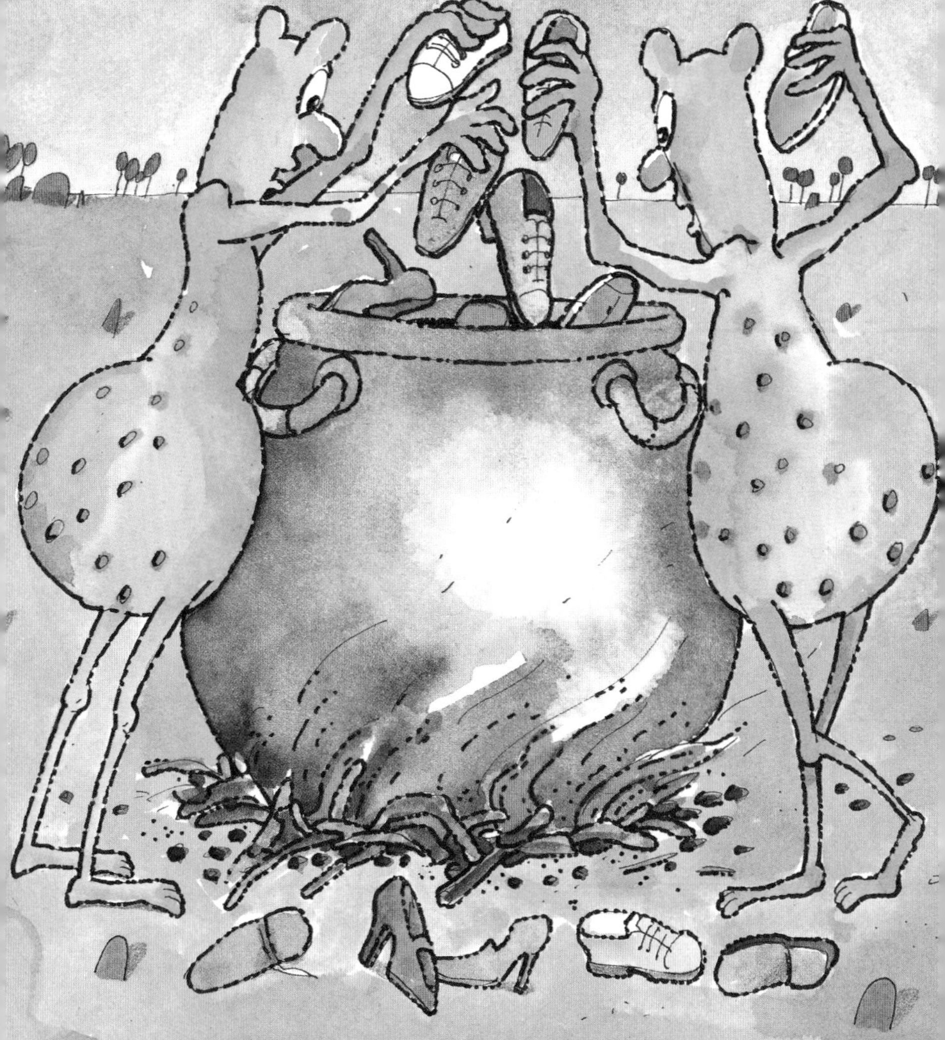

In go some shoes.

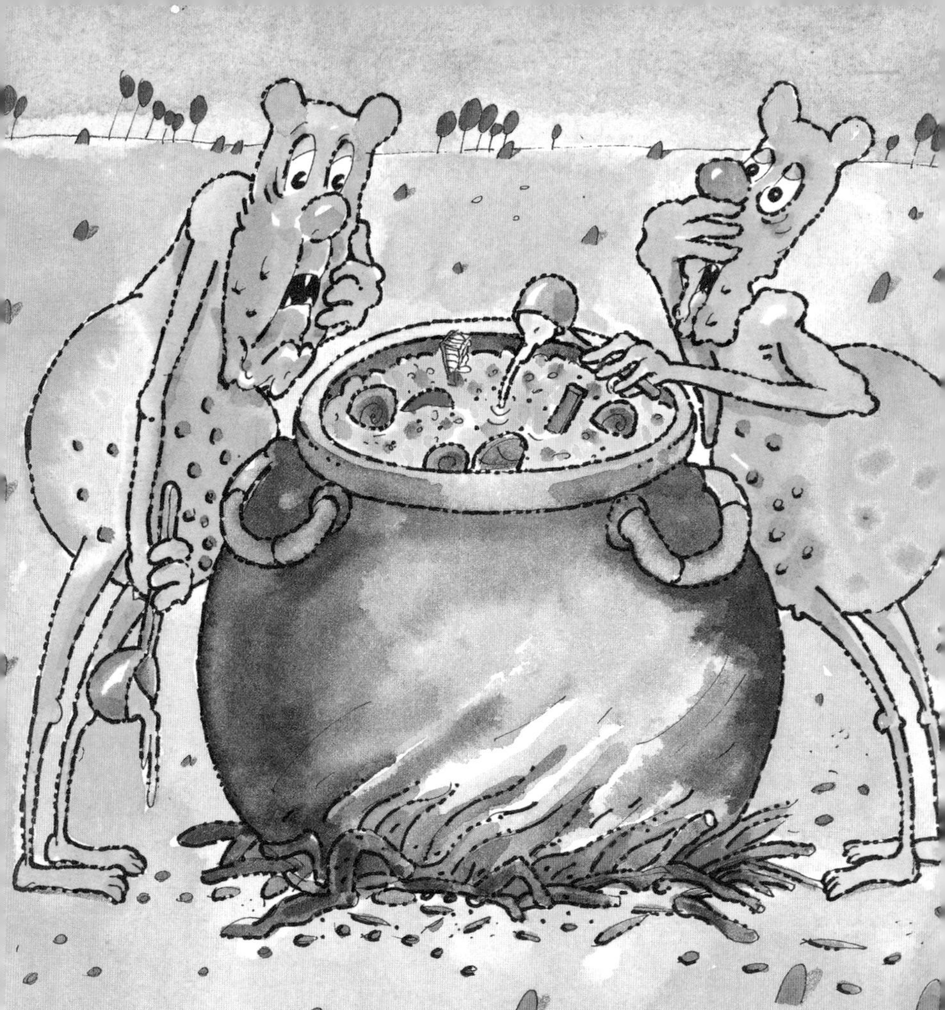

Yuck!